DEC 14

What Lives in the Wetlands?

Oona Gaarder-Juntti

Consulting Editor, Diane Craig, M.A./Reading Specialist

Published by ABDO Publishing Company, 8000 West 78th Street, Edina, Minnesota 55439. Copyright © 2009 by Abdo Consulting Group, Inc. International copyrights reserved in all countries. No part of this book may be reproduced in any form without written permission from the publisher. Super SandCastle™ is a trademark and logo of ABDO Publishing Company.

Printed in the United States.

Credits
Editor: Liz Salzmann
Content Developer: Nancy Tuminelly
Cover and Interior Design and Production: Oona Gaarder-Juntti, Mighty Media
Illustration: Oona Gaarder-Juntti
Photo Credits: Ed George/Getty Images, iStockphoto/Liz Leyden/ Merijn van der Vliet, ShutterStock

Library of Congress Cataloging-in-Publication Data

Gaarder-Juntti, Oona, 1979-

 What lives in the wetlands? / Oona Gaarder-Juntti.

   p. cm. -- (Animal habitats)

 ISBN 978-1-60453-180-0

 1. Wetland animals--Juvenile literature. 2. Wetland ecology--Juvenile literature. I. Title.

 QL113.8.G24 2008

 591.768--dc22

                                       2008016641

Super SandCastle™ books are created by a team of professional educators, reading specialists, and content developers around five essential components— phonemic awareness, phonics, vocabulary, text comprehension, and fluency— to assist young readers as they develop reading skills and strategies and increase their general knowledge. All books are written, reviewed, and leveled for guided reading, early reading intervention, and Accelerated Reader® programs for use in shared, guided, and independent reading and writing activities to support a balanced approach to literacy instruction.

About SUPER SANDCASTLE™

**Bigger Books for Emerging Readers
Grades K–4**

Created for library, classroom, and at-home use, Super SandCastle™ books support and engage young readers as they develop and build literacy skills and will increase their general knowledge about the world around them. Super SandCastle™ books are part of SandCastle™, the leading PreK–3 imprint for emerging and beginning readers. Super SandCastle™ features a larger trim size for more reading fun.

Let Us Know
Super SandCastle™ would like to hear your stories about reading this book. What was your favorite page? Was there something hard that you needed help with? Share the ups and downs of learning to read. We want to hear from you! Send us an e-mail.

sandcastle@abdopublishing.com

Contact us for a complete list of SandCastle™, Super SandCastle™, and other nonfiction and fiction titles from ABDO Publishing Company.

www.abdopublishing.com • 8000 West 78th Street
Edina, MN 55439 • 800-800-1312 • 952-831-1632 fax

Wetlands are areas where the ground is always very wet. The land can also be covered with shallow water. Swamps, bogs, and marshes are all examples of wetlands.

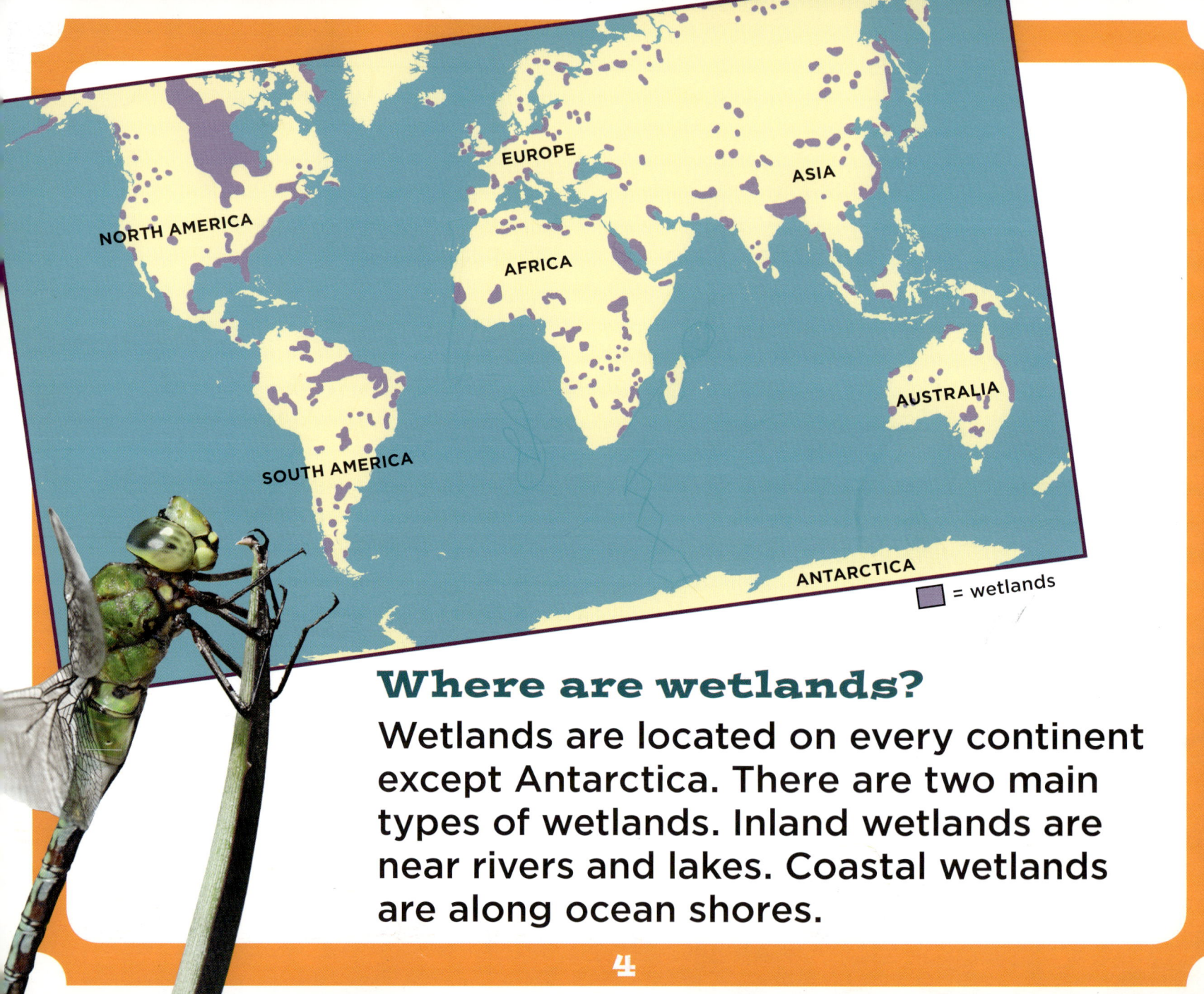

= wetlands

Where are wetlands?

Wetlands are located on every continent except Antarctica. There are two main types of wetlands. Inland wetlands are near rivers and lakes. Coastal wetlands are along ocean shores.

What do wetlands look like?

Wetlands have different zones that range from shallow water to drier land. Many types of animals and plants live in the wetlands.

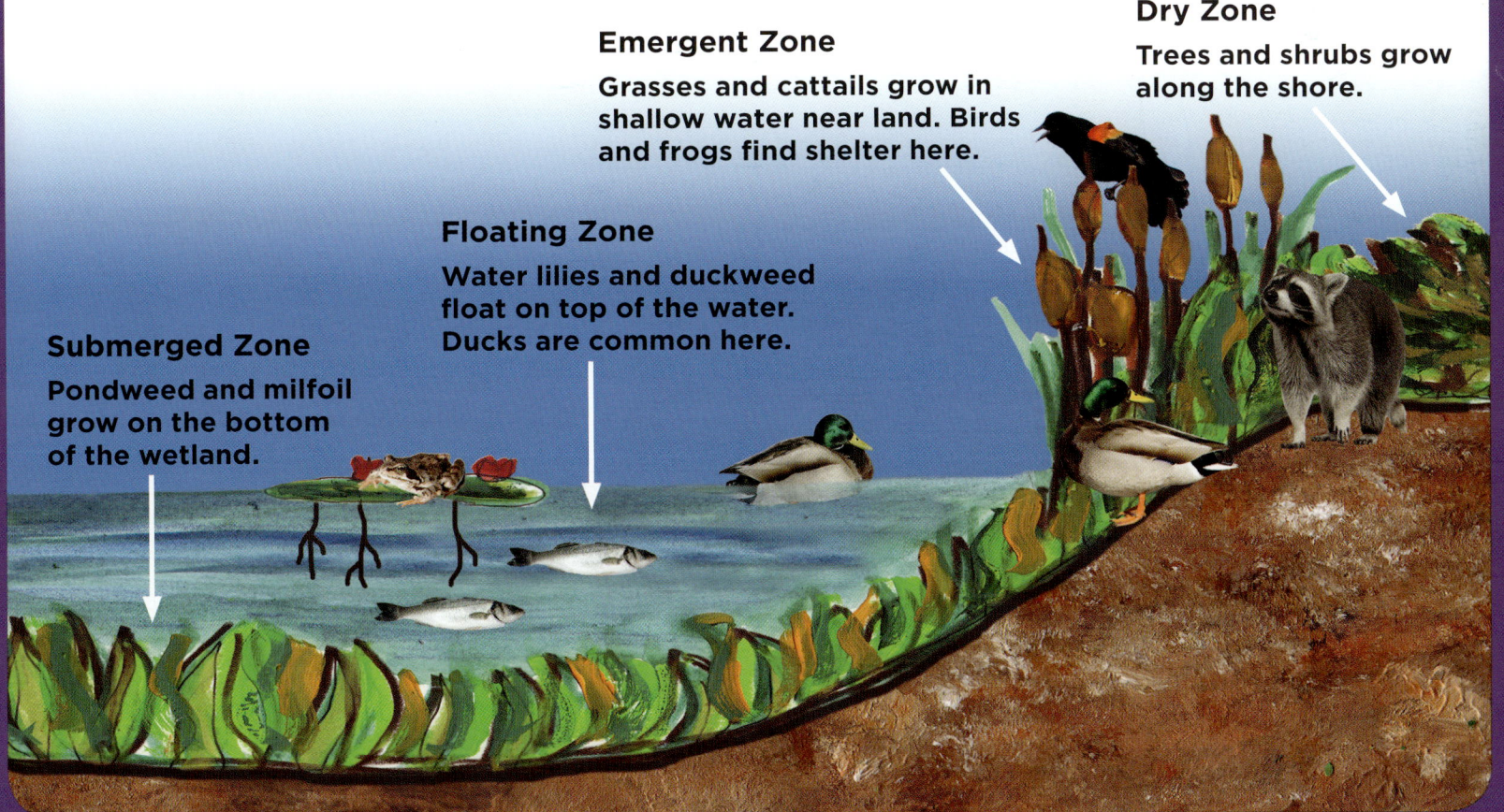

Emergent Zone
Grasses and cattails grow in shallow water near land. Birds and frogs find shelter here.

Dry Zone
Trees and shrubs grow along the shore.

Floating Zone
Water lilies and duckweed float on top of the water. Ducks are common here.

Submerged Zone
Pondweed and milfoil grow on the bottom of the wetland.

Mudskipper

Animal class: Fish
Location: Australia, Africa, and Asia

Mudskippers are fish that can survive out of water. They use their large front fins to walk, jump, swim, and even climb trees.

A mudskipper's eyes are on top of its head. This allows it to see above and below the water at the same time.

7

Painted Turtle

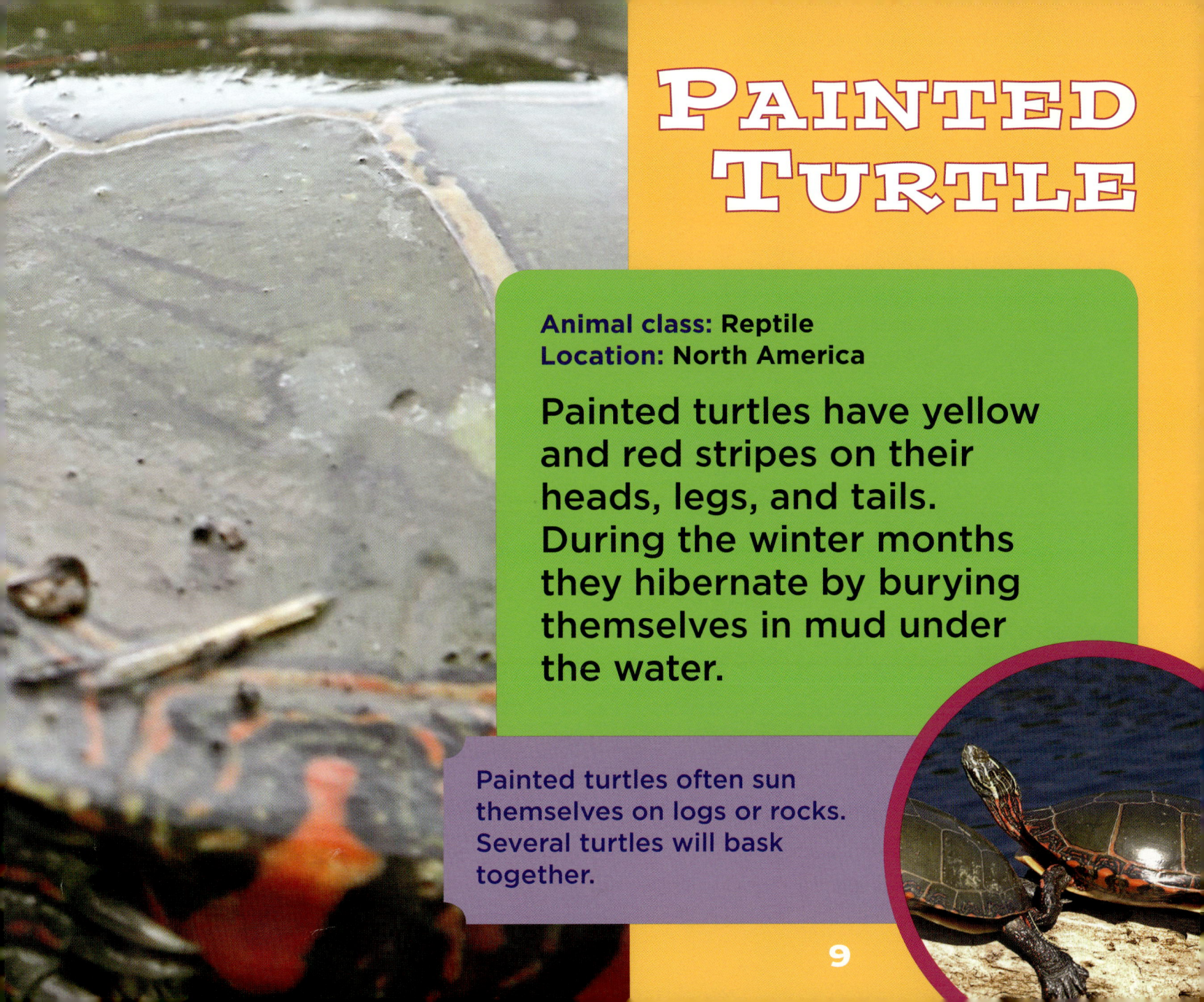

Animal class: Reptile
Location: North America

Painted turtles have yellow and red stripes on their heads, legs, and tails. During the winter months they hibernate by burying themselves in mud under the water.

Painted turtles often sun themselves on logs or rocks. Several turtles will bask together.

Catfish

Animal class: Fish
Location: North America, South America, Europe, Africa, Asia, and Australia

Catfish are named for the long feelers around their mouths that look like cat whiskers. Their feelers have taste buds that help them locate food.

There are about 2,500 different kinds of catfish.

11

Roseate Spoonbill

Animal class: Bird
Location: North America and South America

Roseate spoonbills have long, spoon-shaped bills. They move their bills from side to side in the water to catch food. Spoonbills eat fish, shrimp, snails, and insects.

As soon as a spoonbill feels prey touch its bill, it snaps the bill shut.

CAPYBARA

Animal class: Mammal
Location: South America

Capybaras are the largest rodents in the world. Some weigh more than 100 pounds. Their eyes and noses are high on their heads. This helps them see and breathe while swimming.

Capybaras live in groups of 10 to 20. They eat water plants, fruits, and grasses.

Shoebill

Animal class: Bird
Location: Africa

The shoebill has a large, wide bill with a hooked tip at the end. The hook helps it catch and cut up prey. Shoebills eat turtles, frogs, snakes, snails, and fish.

A shoebill can be more than four feet tall. It has a wingspan greater than seven feet.

Green Anaconda

Animal class: Reptile
Location: South America

Green anacondas are the largest snakes in the world. Some are 30 feet long and 550 pounds. They eat anything they can catch. Their prey includes birds, turtles, fish, and deer.

An anaconda doesn't have to eat for several months after a big meal.

American Alligator

Animal class: Reptile
Location: North America

The American alligator is the largest reptile in North America. Alligators have strong jaws with more than 70 teeth. They eat mainly other reptiles, fish, small mammals, and birds.

A baby alligator stays with its mother for up to two years. A mother alligator will carry her young on her back.

Have you ever been to a wetland?

More Wetland Animals

Can you learn about these wetland animals?

bass
beaver
caiman
Canada goose
crayfish
deer
dragonfly
egret
flamingo
green frog
lungfish

newt
mangrove snapper
mink
monitor lizard
raccoon
red-tailed hawk
scarlet ibis
snail
snapping turtle
striped bass
water bug

GLOSSARY

bask – to enjoy lying or sitting in the sun.

continent – one of seven large land masses on earth. The continents are Asia, Africa, Europe, North America, South America, Australia, and Antarctica.

hibernate – to pass the winter in a deep sleep.

hook – a curved object for catching or pulling something.

mammal – a warm-blooded animal that has hair and whose females produce milk to feed the young.

prey – an animal that is hunted or caught for food.

rodent – a mammal with large, sharp front teeth, such as a rat, mouse, or squirrel.

shrimp – a small shellfish often caught for food.

shrub – a short plant with woody stems.

taste bud – an organ that senses taste. Taste buds are usually on the surface of the tongue.

whisker – one of the long hairs around the mouth of an animal.

wingspan – the distance from one wing tip to the other when the wings are fully spread.

zone – an area that is different from the areas next to it.